A VISIT TO GOLD TOWN

By Heather Hammonds
Illustrations by Elizabeth Botté

Contents

Chapter 1

Gold Town

Dear Grandpa,
Yesterday, our class visited a place called Gold Town.
We went there to learn how people lived,
and looked for **gold**, a long time ago.

Many years ago, gold was found near Gold Town. People rushed from all around the world to look for the gold. This was called a "**gold rush**".

Chapter 2

The Main Street

When we arrived at Gold Town,
we walked along the main street.
Many people were dressed in clothes from the past.
We saw soldiers with red coats and tall hats.

Our teacher took us to the blacksmith's shop.
The **blacksmith** put some metal into a fire.
When the metal was hot and soft, he took it out.
He made it into a horseshoe.

As we came out of the shop,
we saw two horses trotting along Main Street.
They pulled a big carriage.
The driver waved to us as he went past.

Two ladies were riding in the carriage.
They were dressed in beautiful clothes from the past.
The ladies waved, too.

Next, we went to a shop that we all wanted to visit – the Gold Town Sweet Shop.
We watched a lady make some delicious sweets.

There were lots of sweets for sale in the shop.
Our teacher bought some **barley sugar**.
She gave everyone some to try.

Chapter 3

Looking for Gold

We left the main street and went down to a little river.
Long ago, miners used metal pans
to look for gold in the river.
This was called panning for gold.

A man showed us how to pan for gold.
Everyone was given a pan.
We had fun, but we did not find any gold!

We stopped for lunch at an old miner's hut.
A lady dressed in clothes from the past
was cooking some bread over a fire.
The bread was called "**damper**".

We had our lunch alongside the miner's hut.
The lady gave us some damper. It was warm and salty.

Chapter 4

The Gold Town Mine

After lunch, we walked to the Gold Town mine. Lots of gold was found in the mine, during the gold rush.

A guide told us that the mine went a long way under the ground.
There was wood on the sides and roof of the tunnel, to keep it open.

I noticed some miners digging in the tunnel.
At first, I thought they were real people.
Then, I saw that they were part of a display.

In the days of the gold rush, rock was taken out of the mine and crushed by a huge machine.
Sometimes, there was gold inside the rock.

After our visit to the mine,
we went back to the main street.
We saw an old bowling alley.
There were big wooden balls and bowling pins.

I had a turn at bowling. So did my friends.
We tried to knock all of the pins down.

Chapter 5

School Time

Next, we visited the Gold Town school.
We learned about schools during gold rush times.
The school had one big room.
Everyone sat at long, wooden desks.

The first school building in Gold Town was a tent. The teacher and children were very hot in summer and cold in winter.

We wrote some words with a pen and ink. The teacher showed us how to dip our pens into the ink.

Chapter 6

Home Time

Soon, it was time to go home.
Gold Town was a very good place to visit.
I learned many things about
how people lived and mined for gold, long ago.

Love from, Hannah

Glossary

barley sugar *(noun)* a hard yellow or brown boiled sweet

blacksmith *(noun)* a person who makes things by heating and bending metal

damper *(noun)* a kind of bread

gold *(noun)* a yellow metal that is worth a lot of money

gold rush *(noun)* when thousands of people rush to a place to look for gold